The Tale of Caliph Stork

retold by Lenny Hort

from the tale by Wilhelm Hauff

pictures by Friso Henstra

Dial Books for Young Readers *New York*

Published by Dial Books for Young Readers
A Division of Penguin Books USA Inc.
2 Park Avenue, New York, New York 10016

Published simultaneously in Canada
by Fitzhenry & Whiteside Limited, Toronto
Designed by Jane Byers Bierhorst
Printed in Hong Kong
by South China Printing Co.
First Edition
W
1 3 5 7 9 10 8 6 4 2

Library of Congress Cataloging in Publication Data

Hort, Lenny / The tale of Caliph Stork.

From the tale by Wilhelm Hauff.
Summary / When the Caliph of Baghdad finds himself
trapped in the body of a stork, only the evil sorcerer
with designs on his throne knows the magic word that
will restore the Caliph to his human form.
[1. Fairy tales. 2. Folklore—Iraq.]
I. Hauff, Wilhelm, 1802-1827.
II. Henstra, Friso, ill.
III. Title.
PZ8.H788Tal   1989   [398.2]   [E]   87-24511
ISBN 0-8037-0525-5
ISBN 0-8037-0526-3 (lib. bdg.)

The Tale of Caliph Stork is retold from
"Die Geschichte von Kaliph Storch" in the
German author Wilhelm Hauff's book *The Caravan*.

*The art for each picture consists of an
ink and watercolor painting, which is color-separated
and reproduced in full color.*

For Laaren,
my bird of paradise
L.C.H.

—————————————

For Rietje
F.H.

With a servant to fan him and a good hot cup of coffee to drink, Caliph Chasid of Baghdad was utterly content. But Mansor, the Grand Vizier, was restless. "Your Highness," he said, "I just passed a peddler with so many wonderful things in his pack that I kicked myself for not having any money on me."

The Caliph sent a man to fetch the peddler.

Chasid bought gifts for the Vizier and his wife. But what caught his eye was a snuffbox filled with strange dark powder. There was a mysterious inscription on the box. "I have no idea what this is," said the peddler, "so name your price." The Caliph bought the box and sent the peddler on his way.

The Caliph was very curious about the inscription. "My gracious lord," the Vizier said, "a man called Selim the Wise lives near the Grand Mosque. They say he knows all tongues."

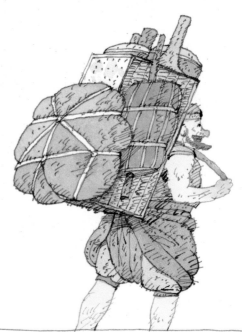

The wise man was summoned. "Selim," said the Caliph, "read me this and I'll see that you get the finest set of clothes of any man in Baghdad. Or don't, and I'll see you whipped for fraud."

Selim said, "Hang me if this isn't Latin. *Let he who finds this praise Allah's grace. Whoever sniffs this powder and says* Mutabor *can change into any animal and understand the tongue of beasts. To regain human form, bow thrice to the east and repeat that word. But beware! He who laughs while under this spell will forget the magic word and remain a beast forever.*"

The Caliph rewarded the wise man and swore him to secrecy.

At dawn the Caliph and Vizier went looking for creatures to transform themselves into. They spotted a stork hunting for frogs in a pond and squawking to itself. Another stork glided down alongside.

"My lord," said the Vizier, "I bet you our long-legged friends are about to chat. What wouldn't you give to be a stork right now?"

"Just remember," said the Caliph as he held out the snuffbox, "three bows to the east, then say *Mutabor* and we're ourselves again. But for heaven's sake don't laugh or we're lost for sure." Each man took a good sniff of powder and called out *Mutabor!*

Their legs shriveled while their feet became long-toed and scaly. Arms became wings as their necks shot high over their shoulders. Hair, beards, and clothes vanished into feathers.

The new-made storks wobbled over toward the real storks and were amazed to hear: "Good morning, Miss Longlegs. You're out early."

"Miss Chatterbeak, so good to see you! I was just getting some breakfast. Won't you have a little lizard or some nice frog foot?"

"Thank you, I couldn't. I have to practice my dancing."

She took some graceful steps. Mansor and Chasid watched with interest. But when she stretched on one leg and circled her wings, they couldn't help themselves. They laughed and laughed.

"That was priceless," the Caliph finally muttered. "Too bad we scared the silly birds off. Maybe she was going to sing."

Then it dawned on the Vizier that laughing was forbidden. "By Mecca and Medina," he cried, "it's no joke if I have to stay a stork! You'd better remember that stupid word because I sure don't."

"We just bow three times to the east and say *Mu-Mu-Mu*."

They bowed till their beaks hit the ground. But alas the magic word had flown from their minds. No matter how earnestly they cried *Mu-Mu-Mu*, storks they were and storks they would remain.

And so they drifted for days. As long as they were storks, there was no going home. Who would accept a stork's claim to the throne? All they could do was hover over the roofs of Baghdad and watch.

One day they saw a solemn funeral and realized that it was for themselves. But the next day there was a great parade. Half the city cried, "Hail, Kaschnur, Lord of Baghdad!"

The two storks stared down until Chasid said, "So my wicked cousin has my throne. And Kaschnur is the most powerful sorcerer I know. He *must* have had something to do with that powder. Come, we'll make a pilgrimage to the Prophet's grave and pray the spell will fade on sacred soil." Off they flew toward the holy city of Medina.

It was not an easy flight for fledgling storks. After two hours they landed at a ruined castle and searched for a place to rest. Suddenly the Vizier froze. "I'd swear I heard something spooky," he whispered.

Now the Caliph heard a cry that sounded almost human. He hurried down a dark hall and pushed open a door.

A large owl sat in the dim light of a bare chamber, weeping. But when she saw the Caliph with the Vizier right behind him, she gave a cry of joy. She gracefully wiped her tears and said in good human Arabic, "Allah be praised! It was prophesied a stork would save me."

The Caliph bowed, amazed. "My dear owl," he said, "it seems you're a fellow victim. But I'm afraid you can't expect much help from us."

When he had told his story, she said, "Now hear a tale just as sad. I'm unlucky Lusa, Princess of India. That sorcerer Kaschnur was my undoing too. He asked for my hand, but my hot-headed father tossed him out. So the wretch disguised himself and served the drink that did this to me. I awoke to the sound of his dreadful words: 'This is how you'll stay, scorned by every living creature, till your last day or till some man freely marries you as you are. I am avenged on you and your proud father.'

"That was months ago. Now I live like a miserable hermit, blinded by anything brighter than moonlight." She wiped away tears.

"Unless I'm mistaken," the Caliph remarked, "there's a single answer to your problem and ours."

The owl replied, "I'm sure of it. A wise woman once said that a stork would bring me luck, and now I understand. I know a hall where that sorcerer meets his companions. They're always bragging about dastardly deeds. Somebody might let slip that magic word you've forgotten."

"My dearest princess," gasped the Caliph, "where is this hall and when do they go there?"

The owl paused and said, "I can tell you only if one of you pledges me your hand in marriage."

The Caliph beckoned his minister aside. "My dear Vizier," he whispered, "you have the chance to do me and your country a great service."

"Sure, and have my wife scratch my eyes out when I get home. Besides I'm an old man, but you're young and rich and single and just perfect for a beautiful young princess."

"And what makes you so sure she's young and beautiful?" The Caliph sighed, his wings drooping. "Talk about a bird in the bush!"

They argued, but the Caliph finally accepted the fact that the Vizier would rather stay a stork than marry the owl. He agreed to do it himself, and she told them that the sorcerer's banquet would take place that very night in those very ruins.

She led the storks to a place where they were able to peer in at feasting men, joined by a man in rags—the peddler who had sold the magic powder. "Alms for the poor," he said.

"How in Allah's name did this rogue get in here?" asked someone at the table.

"Go," said another, tossing the peddler some bread. "If our master finds you, he'll turn you into a toad."

"Who is this master?" asked the peddler. And then he tore off his own beard. He pulled off his nose. He took a large cushion out from under his tunic and tossed it, laughing, at the men at the table.

Those men were bowing. "Master!" they cried.

And the storks and the owl saw that it was treacherous Kaschnur himself.

"Relax, my friends, for you are no more foolish than the Caliph of Baghdad," the sorcerer said as he sat down to feast. And at length he told them all about his trickery.

"What sort of magic word did you use?" one of them asked.

"Something Latin he won't stumble on in a million years."

"What word was that?" asked a voice.

"It was *Mutabor*," mumbled Kaschnur carelessly. He went on talking, not realizing that it was the Caliph himself who had called out the question.

Once outside the Caliph took the owl by the wing and said, "We can never repay you, but please be my wife." The storks bowed three times toward the rising sun. *Mutabor!* they cried, and became two men laughing and weeping for joy. But who was the beautiful lady?

"Don't you recognize your night owl?" Princess Lusa asked. The Caliph was so taken with her that he swore becoming a stork was the best thing that had ever happened to him.

Soon they were back in Baghdad. The people were overjoyed to have their beloved master back. A mob seized Kaschnur and brought him before the Caliph. Chasid let his cousin choose between the gallows and the magic powder. One good sniff, and the secret word turned him into a peacock. One good laugh at the hands of the royal tickler, and he stayed that way. The Caliph kept him caged in the garden.

Caliph Chasid and his bride shared a long and happy life. He often talked with his faithful Vizier about their days as storks. The Caliph would even imitate the way they had looked in feathers. Legs rigid, he would flap his arms and bow over and over, crying *Mu-Mu-Mu*. The princess and her children loved these performances, but sometimes he went on so long that the Vizier lost his patience and threatened to reveal just what Caliph Stork had said about marrying Princess Night Owl.